To Evie Stack, my little honey that's always buzzing!

Evie Bee can  and fly,
Evie Bee can touch the sky,

Evie Bee can **ZOOM** and flutter,
Evie Bee is like no other!

She can wiggle and she can squirm,
She can dance so we can learn,

Where to find her favorite flower,
Never wilting, never dour.

She ' ll lead us there in queued parades,
To fields colored bright just like arcades,

We'll play in pollen, our faces sunny,
And later shake and make some honey!

But when the clouds get gray and grumpy,
And when the sky gets dark and dumpy,

And when the rain begins to drop,
We'll race back home until it stops.

Then when the sun comes back out to play,
We'll leave the hive and shout "Hurray!"

With new light brings us new chances,
To make our honey and practice our dances!

Whether the sky is bright or stormy,
Whether you just won it all or lost it sorely,

It makes no difference about the weather,
Nothing lasts the same forever.

So treat each day that comes as passing,
Let loose the rain, enjoy the dancing,

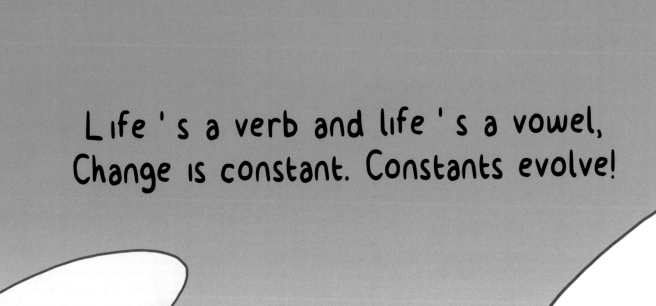

Life 's a verb and life 's a vowel,
Change is constant. Constants evolve!

Made in the USA
Middletown, DE
05 October 2023